"The Adventures of Dan Lewis and Clark Hamilton," by Phillips Wylly. ISBN 978-1-63868-127-4 (softcover).

Published 2023 by Virtualbookworm.com Publishing Inc., P.O. Box 9949, College Station, TX 77842, US.

The Adventures

Dan

LEWIS and CLA

Han

A Short Story
by
Phillips Wylly

Large Print

Dedicated to:
Bobby Bernshausen,
Virtalbookworm Publishing

Your company and your support have made my life as a would-be author great fun.

Thank you, Bobby.

Ladies and Gentlemen, for your 4th of July pleasure, Aronstein's Famous Catskills Resort proudly takes you Across the Wide Missouri."

As the applause diminishes, a tall, handsome, dark haired young man wearing casual wear and carrying a guitar, strolls out onto the stage and begins to sing.

"Hey! Hey vhat's goin' on here?" The singer tries to ignore the annoying voice from the audience... "Far above the shining waters..."

"Stop! Stop aw-ready." The voice would not be ignored. "It says here 'comedy'." A man seated at one of the third-row tables gets to his feet waving a copy of the show program. "Not sing-ging. Comedy. You ain't funny. Me, I'm even funnier dan you."

"Sir...." The heckler could no longer be ignored. "Sir... please." The singer looks hopelessly at the audience seeking support that seems somewhat lacking. Well, if you can't lick 'em, join 'em, he decided.

"Okay," he turned towards the heckler. "You're funny, are ya?" Looking up at the spotlight booth he points towards his antagonist, "Put a light on that guy fellas."

A spotlight beam finds the heckler. A tall, very slender, rubbery faced young man wearing a tuxedo and a Yarmulke, standing on his chair with his right arm somehow wrapped around the back of his neck so that the fingers on his hand were looking into his eye.

The singer calls to him, "Okay wise guy, tell us a joke."

"Aw-wight," the heckler answers in almost baby talk. Then, speaking to the hand that is in front of his face, "Da man wants a joke, so... What did the little egg say to the chic-un out dere in da lobby?"

The hand makes a motion that indicates it has no idea what the egg might have said to the chicken.

"Vell..." The heckler speaks slowly, carefully as one might to a child, "The little egg said... Now dat you laid me here in the lobby, you gunna call me ven ya get back ta da city?"

The laughter that shook the tired old wooden rafters of Aronstein's Show Room was loud and prolonged.

"All right." The singer wipes laughter's tears from his eyes and tries to regain his composure. "All right Lewis. Get your tucas up here!"

As "the heckler" climbs down off his chair and starts up onto the stage, the off-stage announcer proclaims, "Ladies and Gentlemen, Dan Lewis and Clark Hamilton…"

For the next hour the two tell stories, discuss politics and do bits of "slapstick" comedy. Clark Hamilton sings in a very pleasing baritone voice while Danny Lewis mugs, tap dances, does flip flops, and the audience seldom stops laughing.

PART I: When Eve lit the Light

Monday morning, Fred Young walked into the RCA Building's 23rd floor offices of Stacey/Conners Productions and stuck his head into Eve Light's office. He knew she would be there. He had long ago given up any thought of beating her to the office on Monday mornings. Besides, he didn't have to be there first. He was the boss... except for Chuck and Cathy of course... and Franko and Peatro Tucci, and Hugh Crawford.

Every now and then he had to pinch himself to make sure it wasn't all a dream. One day he had been sitting in his crummy little office on 48th Street booking musicians and the next day he was the president of

Stacey/Connors Productions, managing the band and making deals for them. That was more than twenty years ago, before Cathy left to make her way in the film world and before Peatro Tucci became Peter Best. It was before the TV show, before Chuck and Cathy finally got married, before they bought the film studio and he became president of StayCon Pictures as well. And now it seemed the damn studio was taking up more of his time than anything else. Thank God for Eve, he often told himself.

Eve Light had come to work for him as an "assistant everything" when the Chuck Stacey Show first went on television as a summer replacement. And the thing of it was, Eve didn't look any different today than she did in ten years ago.

She was small, maybe five foot three, she had brown hair, a pretty face and a great body. Best of all was her personality. She was bright, funny, caring, you name it, if it's a complimentary adjective, it fit her. And she was smarter than any woman he had ever known. On second thought, he didn't know why he limited it to women. She was smarter than just about anybody, man or woman, and she was an indispensable part of the team. About the only thing that had changed over the years was her marriage to a quiet, unassuming man named Harvey Morton, a poet who made his living as the writer of weekly financial column for the Wall Street Journal.

Fred opened the door to her office and walked in. "So how was the vacation?"

"Vacation?" Eve tried not to laugh. "A three-day Fourth of July weekend he calls a 'vacation. Mister Young, a vacation is when Harvey and I take a month off and go to the Bahamas."

“Don’t hold your breath,” Fred laughed as he went to the coffee maker she always kept at the ready and poured himself a cup. “Want a refill?” He held up the pot and looked towards her.

“Yes, please, then come sit down. I’ve got to tell you about an act we saw at Aronstein’s.”

“So you vent up ta-da Catskills aw-ready?” Fred tried his Yiddish accent which never fit his natural New York Irish too well.

“To Aronstein’s,” Eve agreed. “And we saw this act, ‘Lewis and Clark‘. Fred, they brought the house down.”

“So when are they gonna be on the show?”

“That’s what I want to talk to you about. No one has ever heard of them, but I'd like to give them a spot on the show. Fact is..." Eve hesitated for a moment. A calculated hesitation to make sure Fred was tuned in.

"Yes?... He was.

"I want to change our show format."

"This sounds serious." Fred sat down.

Eve took a deep breath, "Every year our first show has featured a top act from last year. But here it is nineteen fifty-eight. It's time for a change. Come September we will be in color and I want our opener to feature a brand new act. An act no one every heard of before and Lewis and Clark will be a knock out!"

"Oh my..." Fred scratched his chin

"What'a you think?" Eve asked him.

Fred scratched his chin again, picked up his coffee, stood, and walked to the door to Eve's office where he read the information discreetly printed there. "Eve Light, Producer." He turned back towards her, "So vhat-chu asking me for?"

"Because on your door it says President," she called after his disappearing, rather broad rear end.

A moment later he reappeared, "What the hell Eve. Just because Cathy and Chuck set the show format doesn't mean they will be upset by some hair brain idea like that but there is no point asking me. Format changes are way above my pay grade, Call Cathy. Call Chuck.

"Thanks Fred," she called after him. "That's just what I'm gonna do!".

Half an hour later Eve knocked on Fred's door than pushed it open. "I just got off the phone with Chuck and Cathy. They think it's a great idea. I told them you were not in favor of it and Chuck just said, "Oh really?"

Fortunately, there was nothing on Fred's desk for him to throw at her.

“Molly Loubowski, please,” Eve told the voice that answered her phone call to the Loubow Agency.

“This is Molly,” the voice replied. A happy voice, Eve thought.

“Miss Loubowski, this is Eve Light. I’m with Stacey/Conners Productions. We do the Chuck and Cathy Television Show.”

“My God, I may be in Brooklyn booking the borsch belt, but I know already Stacey/Conners Productions. You’re da producer, right?”

“Yes, I am,” Eve laughed, you had to like this woman. “And I’m calling because I saw one of your acts at Aronstein's the other night and I want to book them for our show."

There was a slight gasp at the other end of the line before Molly Loubowiski's voice stammered, "My son, da comic?"

"Your son?" Eve wasn't exactly certain what the woman was asking.

"Yeah. My son Danny. He's da 'Lewis' in Lewis and Clark. That's the act at Aronstein's."

"That's the act all right," Eve agreed. "I didn't know he's your son, but I certainly know he is a funny man. And his partner. Not only a great straight man but a really good singer."

"Him I never notice," Molly snickered at her own joke, then, "Seriously, you saw their act and you liked it?"

“Very much,” Eve told her. “I think they’re great and I know our audience will love ‘em. We start our new season September 6th, right after Labor Day. I would like to book them for that show. Could that work?”

“Dey just happen to be available on dat date.”

“Good,” Eve laughed again. “We’ll be in touch.”

One of Eve’s primary rules regarding the care and feeding of show talent was the personal touch. Contracts were always sent to their agents as soon as a deal was agreed on and Eve always called to be sure they arrived, and, frequently at her gentle insistence, Chuck Stacey himself, would make welcoming calls to the talent a few days later.

DAN LEWIS and CLARK HAMILTON sat looking at each other and the telephone. Dan's mother had told them Chuck Stacey would call them between five and five-thirty. It was now ten minutes after five.

The phone rang.

Both men reached for it but Dan was quicker. Also more nervous. He knocked the phone to the floor.

"Relax, Danny," Clark told him as he reached for the phone.

"Yeah. Yeah. You talk to him. I'm too nervous."

"Hello Mister Stacey, this is Clark Hamilton."

There was a chuckle from the other end of the line followed by that unmistakable voice, "You guys clairvoyant too?"

"No sir," Clark smiled. "It's just that after I dumped my latest chick, we changed our phone number and you're the only person who has the new one."

"Ummm. I guess the pickings are pretty good up there in the mountains."

"Every week a new crop." Clark assured him.

"Sounds good. Is your partner there?"

"Yeah, I'll put him on." Clark handed the phone to Danny, "Say hello to the boss."

Hi Mister Stacey." There was no sign of nervousness in his voice now. "It's a real thrill to talk to you and I can't begin to tell you how much we appreciate the chance to be on your show."

The three exchanged a few more pleasantries, Chuck told them he looked forward to meeting them in person at the show rehearsal and they said good-bye.

"It's real," Dan said as he switched off. "It's real, Clark. We are going to be on the Chuck and Cathy Show. Do you realize what this can mean to us?"

"Yeah, yeah." Clark nodded his head up and down. "It could give us a real boost." Clark stood up, stretched and started towards the door. "OK, I'm gonna have a little something to eat with Zoe. I'll see ya at show time."

Unbelievable! Dan Lewis sat there shaking his head as his partner disappeared. They had just been talking with Mr. Television. The man himself. The man who's show could catapult them into the big time and Clark was just about as excited as if someone had offered to put an extra cherry in his cream soda.

"The fucking guy lives in a world of his own," he said out loud It gave him a headache just thinking about it. It gave him indigestion too.

He stood up and walked to the room window. The sun was about to set and it was casting beautiful, long, shadows across the hillside behind the building. The Catskills were so soft and beautiful at this time in the evening, in fact he found them beautiful at any time. He loved to hike in the mountains but beautiful mountains didn't help tonight and God Damn Clark Hamilton didn't either!

What he needed was a couple aspirin and a Tums. Fuck the mountains!

CLARK HAMILTON grew up on Long Island in the little town of Port Washington. Clark's father was a conductor on the Long Island Railroad. His mother was a telephone operator. She had always liked to sing and sang in the church choir every Sunday. From his birth she had sung to Clark and encouraged him to sing with her, which accounted for half his performing talent, the other half was courtesy of the Port Washington Public School's Music Program. Starting in third grade, students were encouraged to take up a musical instrument. The school provided instruments as well as lessons. Clark and a guitar quickly found each other.

Playing the guitar and singing at High School Assembly Programs together with his good looks made him very appealing to the young ladies in his class. A fact his father became aware of when evening phone calls were frequently for his son. This resulted in a 16th Birthday gift of a package on condoms and pamphlet dealing with sexual activity.

One more thing about Clark: he was very smart; usually at the top of his class which had resulted in a Scholarship at NYU.

DANIEL LOUBOWSKI was born in Brooklyn, New York. His mother. Molly. had been a show dancer. He did not know his father. He was never sure his mother knew just who he was either. Perhaps the lack of a father was the reason for his lack of sexuality. He just did not want to father a child and not even know him...or her.

Becoming pregnant had ended Molly's dancing career and the Loubow Agency was born. Finding work for others was far less difficult than trying to perform herself and sitting in an office gave her more time to be with her son who meant everything to her.

He was not yet three when his double-jointed arms became apparent as he reached around behind his head to scratch his right ear with his left hand while putting food in his mouth with his right, and Molly knew who her most important client would someday be and to that day she worked with him constantly:

Tap dancing: His double joints quickly led to high in the air flips.

Ventriloquism: Soon his right fist, "Thummy," was talking to him.

While he was still in High School Molly had him performing in local Night Clubs. Thing was, he did well in school, too. And doing well in school led to a scholarship at NYU.

Clark and Dan met their freshman year at NYU when they found themselves sitting next to each other in a

Political Science class. Clark loved Political Science. Just what the hell he was doing in a PoliSci class Dan didn't know. He guessed it was fate. The two hit it off right from that first day. Clark had done half his homework for him and tutored him to a B average in the class. Of course, Clark had gotten straight A's.

He learned that Clark liked to sing and since he was trying his wings at comedy in clubs over in Brooklyn, where his mother could book him, he suggested that they team up. "We'll call ourselves 'Lewis and Clark'. It's a natural!"

Living in Brooklyn while going to college in New York City, "Dan Lewis" spent many hours on subway trains, but he never felt really comfortable being underground. Such was the case today as he and Clark headed for the 47th Street Theatre, home of the Chuck and Cathy Show. Finally reaching the 48th Street station each step up to street level made him feel better. At last, daylight. Then a short two block walk took them to…

"Wait a second, Clark." Dan put his hand on his partner's arm as he looked up at the theatre marquee:

48th Street Theatre

The

CHUCK and CATHY

SHOW

"Our future is waiting for us in there."

And for once Clark was serious too. "Yeah. You're right. Let's give it our best shot."

And the "best shot" was very, very good.

———

Standing in front of the orchestra Cathy and Chuck took their usual positions behind a tom tom.

"I guess that's about it for tonight," Chuck said to Cathy as he began lightly playing on the tom tom.

"I guess," Cathy answered. "Tell you one thing though, when we have those two back on the show, I'm going to insist Clark do a song with me."

"Oh?" Chuck cocked his eyebrow as he began beating louder, "We'll talk about that," then, looking directly into the camera, "Good night everybody Hope we see you again next week."

"...And go to black." Director Arthur Rosenblum brought his right arm down in a slow arc indicating the speed at which he wanted the picture to fade out.

Thank you everyone. An outstanding show tonight."

"Yes, thank you, thank you, thank you." Eve Light stood in front of her producer's chair in the row just above and behind the director.

"That really was a great show, Art. I watched all the rehearsals but... Lewis and Clark, I still nearly wet my pants."

"You're not the only one babe." Art grinned back at her. "Those two guys are something else!"

Moments later, back in their dressing room, Cathy looked at her husband who was seated in front of his dressing table but making no effort to remove his stage makeup. “Penny for your thoughts.”

“Are you kidding? My thoughts are worth at least two-bits.”

"That’s pretty steep. I’ll make it a dime, but that’s tops.”
“Well, I am thinking about Lewis and Clark and about coincidences,” Chuck said slowly. “If Eve hadn’t just happened to go up to the Catskills, she would not have discovered them and who knows if anyone else ever would have. That made me think of a night in Chicago a long time ago when I just happened to be sittin’ in and you and your father just happened to stop in.”

Cathy stopped whatever she was doing and sat down in her husband’s lap. “Yes, I guess it was a long time ago, but it seems like only yesterday.” She kissed his cheek. “I love you.”

"And I love you. I just hope those two will have success as we have."

"Are you kidding?" She laughed, "With Eve and Peter pushing 'em how can they lose?"

“**Molly Loubowski, please,”** a pleasant, but formal female voice came over the telephone. “Peter Best calling.”

“This is Molly. You said Peter Best is calling me?”

“Yes. One moment please.”

“Mrs. Loubowski, good morning... I guess it’s afternoon your time...”

“Peter Best?” Molly’s tone indicated her surprise.

“Hollywood’s Best, Peter Best?”

“Yes,” Peter laughed. “Guilty.”

"Oy!" After a pause of several seconds, Molly continued, "So vhat can I do for you Mr. Best?"

"I want to talk to you about Lewis and Clark, Mrs. Loubowski..."

"Look, Mr. Best. Foist ting, better you should call me "Molly" like everyone else. Mrs. Loubowski makes me noyvus."

"Okay, that's a deal if you'll call me Peter."

"Sure. So, Peter, vhat's up?"

"Well, last night's TV show was a success for the boys. I think they have a great future and I would like my agency to represent them here on the west coast. We would share commissions of course. Together I think we can put them on top of the world."

Molly Loubowski had played in a very tough ballpark for a number of years. A ballpark where getting screwed was an almost daily occurrence. The idea that a big agent like Peter Best wanted to help reminded her of other offers she had received over the years.

“Peter, that sounds interesting, but I need to think about that.”

“…All right…” Peter paused briefly, then added, “Is there a problem?”

“A problem? No, not exactly.” Peter noticed Molly’s voice had become less Jewish and more business-like. “The thing is, Mr. Best, this morning I have offers from three night clubs and I promised Eve Light another TV show. I don’t know why I would want to share commissions.”

“Well, assuming those are all firm commitments, I can understand your reluctance," Peter's voice had also become more business like, "But there's a big world beyond those dates. You should think about it, and talk with the boys. I really think we can help you with their future. Let me know if you change your mind, Molly

The phone went dead before she could reply and Molly was about to learn the telephone is sometimes not a friend.

The next morning the telephone on Eve Light's secretary's desk rang and a voice she recognized said, "This is Molly. May I speak to Eve please, Joanie."

"One minute please, Mrs. Loubowski. Let me see if she's in her office, she may have gone down the hall to talk with Mr. Stacey."

Molly waited. After several seconds Eve came on the line. “Hello Molly. How are you?” Molly thought Eve’s voice sounded a little strained. “I’ve been meaning to call, but I have been up to my ears...”

“Busy, I can believe,” Molly told her. “Producing a TV Show every week.” She hesitated for a moment, then continued, “I vouldn’t keep you, I just want to check on the October date. I didn’t get the contract yet and I had some inquiries from a couple clubs...”

“Oh Molly, I’m glad you called. You are on my list to get to this week. We are going to have to put off that date, the network has decided they want to do a football special.”

“Mr. Walters, Molly Loubowski calling, Lewis and Clark. I want to let you know the boys could be available for you in October…"

"Molly. How nice of you to call. Gee, I wish I'd known sooner. I just signed another deal for those dates. Maybe we can do something later in the fall."

———

"Mr. Sapolo, I was expecting the schedule in the mail today. Is something wrong maybe?"

"Molly, how can I tell you this? It's so embarrassing. Our owner is insisting we put another act into those dates we talked about. I meant to call you yesterday…"

———

"Eve please, Joanne. This is Molly again…"

"I'm sorry Mrs. Loubowski, she's tied up in a meeting. Can I have her get back to you?"

Heading for home, after a long, busy day, Eve stepped off the elevator and found herself face to face with Molly Loubowski.

"Eve, I think you're my friend; I can't get chu on da phone and I need to talk to you."

"Molly…" Eve blinked, looked quickly from side to side, then took Molly's arm. "Come on. We can't talk here. I know a restaurant that's out of the way."

Call it luck, call it a fluke, call it just plain amazing, there was an empty taxicab waiting in front of the RCA

Building's 50th Street entrance. The two climbed in and spoke of things like the weather and the new boots smart women were wearing until they reached 3rd Avenue and 58th Street and were seated at the rear of "Original Joe's"

Eve took the lead and ordered Manhattans for both of them, then turned to Molly. "Okay, I can guess why we're here but why don't you tell me anyway."

"Eve. What did you get us into? The boys were on top of the world. Your show. Clubs all over the country. Suddenly I can't even get my phone calls answered."

"Really...?"

"Eve. Please don't play games wid me. You're too smart. You know vhat's going on. So tell me. Is it Peter Best?"

"Peter Best? The agent...?" Eve glanced away from Molly and looked down at the sea of little white octagonal tiles that made up the floor of Original Joe's.

She did not like this part of the business. She knew not everything was straight arrow, true blue in any business; certainly not in the entertainment business where she had spent all of her adult life. And it wasn't as if she had never played games herself, but that didn't mean she liked doing it. She particularly disliked doing it to Molly Loubowski. She had become fond of Molly and knew Molly had not enjoyed an easy life.

"Eve..."

Before Molly could continue the waiter arrived with their drinks. She took a large sip before continuing. "Eve. You and me... it's business, but a little bit we're friends. If it weren't for you, my Danny and da sing-ga vould still be voik-king Aronstein's. From you dey become big stars. "Den Mr. Best calls. He vants a piece-a-da action. I tell him I don't tink so and suddenly dere ain't no action."

Molly made a second pass at her drink, this time finishing it off. Holding up the empty glass she signaled their waiter to bring her a refill.

"Eve. I'm sure you know dis. Vhat should I do?"

Following Molly's lead, Eve finished her Manhattan before she tried to answer.

"Molly," she began slowly. "Every week I have to book six or seven big name acts for our show." She put her hand on Molly's arm and waited while their waiter delivered Molly's drink. "I'll have another one too," she told him, then turned back to Molly. “About half those acts are represented by the Best Agency.”

Molly straightened in her chair and looked into Eve’s eyes. “So you telling me vid out Peter Best you couldn’t do da show?”

“It would be tough Molly. Very tough.”

“So dis Peter Best told you not to book Lewis and Clark?”

“No. I haven’t spoken to him about them. But Peter is very well connected and maybe he spoke to my boss and my boss suggested we shouldn’t bring them back right now.”

“And he would talk to Mr. Walters? And to Carmine Sapolo in Vegas?”

“I have no idea...”

“But those people, they also book acts from Best?”

“Ummm, probably. I would think so.”

“So, Eve. What do I do?”

“If I were you, Molly, I’d call Peter back and tell him you have reconsidered.”

“Oy.”

“Molly, I know Peter Best. He isn’t a bad man. With him, you and the boys will make more money than you ever thought possible.”

“Oy vey.”

THE MORNING AFTER Molly contacted Peter Best to tell him she had reconsidered, she received an unexpected call from Dominic Luciano of The Florenza.

Located not far from the Boston Gardens, The Florenza was perhaps the best know night spot between New York City and Montreal, Canada. Of course she knew of the club and she had heard Luciano's name, but she had never before had any contact with him.

"Molly, you don-a mind I call-a you dat..." he spoke with a definite Italian accent.

“Vhy vould I mind?” Molly laid on the Jewish. “Molly’s da name. And you? I should maybe call you Domonic?”

“Just Dom, will do,” he chuckled. “Like-a Dom DiMaggio.”

“You play baseball?”

“Yeah, I pitch but I’m off today so I’m working the club.”

“Oy, Two jobs yet...”

“So, Molly. What I’m- callin’ for. We just-a had a big act drop out, an’ I need a headliner for nex-a week. I unner-stan your Lewis an-a Clark might be available?”

The three-week booking Luciano offered was at more than twice the money the team had previously been paid.

An even bigger surprise came just before lunch time:

“Loubowski Agence. Dis is Molly.”

“Mrs. Loubowski?”

A soft, very cultured voice sounded in her ear. Time to ease up on the Jewish she told herself “Yes, this is Molly Loubowski, who’s calling please?”

“Mrs. Loubowski, this is Carlton Abbot, Junior, from Oakwood Records.”

Carlton Abbot she didn’t know; Oakwood Records she did. Oakwood was maybe the biggest company in the record business. “Mr. Abbot. Its-a pleasure to talk wid-chu.”

“Thank you, Mrs. Loubowski. I’m calling to inquire about your client Clark Hamilton. If he is not already signed to a recording contract, I would very much like to talk about one with you."

For a brief moment, Molly wasn't quite certain how to respond. Then she realized she didn't have to. She had a partner who should handle this.

"Mr. Abbot, I don't know from recording contracts. My partner, Peter Best, handles that. He's in LA. Can I give you dat number?"

"Oh that isn't necessary, we know Mr. Best quite well. I didn't know you and he are partners though."

"Only for Lewis and Clark," she told him quickly.

———

That afternoon when a contract from Eve's office for an October TV date arrived by Special Delivery Molly slowly looked around her.

“Maybe this office on Bedford Avenue isn’t big enough for the Loubow Agency anymore”, she said to herself.

PART II: What Peter does Best

PETER BEST put his arms around his wife and pulled her close. "What-a-ya say we leave the kids with Nanny for a night or two and go have some fun in Vegas?"

"Just for fun?" The twinkle in her eye told him she was much too smart to be fooled. "Or would it have something to do with Lewis and Clark?"

"Well, they are playing at the Sirocco, and it might be a good idea to catch their act..."

"Umm-Humm."

She smiled, then stood on her tip toes to give him a quick kiss before agreeing, "Sure, it might be a lot of fun. When do you want to go?"

"Tomorrow OK?"

"Tomorrow's perfect."

———

For Lewis and Clark, headlining in the Main Show Room at the Fabulous Sirocco Hotel was wondrously different from doing a show in the Lounge. For one thing the lounge accommodated about two hundred people, the main showroom seated nearly ten times that many. In the lounge they just went out and did their act. In the main room they were surrounded with production:

A seventeen-piece orchestra:

Twelve beautiful dancers:

A juggler:

And a hilarious dog act in which the dog never did anything his trainer asked him to.

Different in other ways, too. Most important, their rate had climbed to five times what it had been. Another important difference, in the main room the shows went on at seven and eleven-thirty, giving Clark an entire night for romance.

Making this evening more special than most, Peter Best and his wife Marion were in the audience. Peter's secretary had telephoned that afternoon to let Clark and Dan know he was going to see the first show and would like to meet with them afterwards.

Jesus, Clark, it's about time!" Dan Lewis looked at his wristwatch. "We go on in twenty minutes, Peter Best is in the audience and you're nowhere around. Where the hell you been?"

"Don't get your balls in an uproar Danny. I had a little business to take care of. We got plenty-a time."

"Business," Dan repeated disgustedly. Clark Hamilton had his English father's name, but he got his devil with the ladies good looks and his laid back charm from his Italian mother.

"A blonde or a brunette?" Dan asked. There was an abundance of both in Las Vegas.

"Well, as a matter of fact she's sort of a red head." Clark smiled a wicked smile as he indicated shapely female curves with his hands. "Real dark red. Auburn. We had a very meaningful discussion about the erection... Election! I mean, election! I think I'm gonna marry her."

"Yeah. Right." Dan shook his head from side to side. What can you do with a guy like this? Women throw themselves at him and he has a perfect fielding average. Maybe he was a bit jealous. But still that feeling of having children you never even knew....

"So ya gunna change or workt like that?"

"Don't worry." Clark pulled off the sweater he was wearing and tossed it onto the chair in the corner of their dressing room. "I'll be ready."

No kidding, Dan thought as he watched his partner pull off his trousers and get into his tuxedo, Clark is really something. Mister Calm. He wished he had Clark's temperament. In a little more than two months they had gone from the Catskills to a TV show appearance and now Las

Vegas. It didn't seem fair Clark could be so at ease while he was so overwhelmed and up tight and nervous.

"Okay, partner, time to get goin'." Clark's easy voice broke into his reverie. "You wanna puke, or are you ready to work?"

"Go fuck yourself, Clark." Dan tried to grin but then, all of a sudden, he did have to puke. Nerves! Shit, why did he have to have nerves? Why couldn't he just relax and walk out there and go to work like Clark did?

Ooopsss...

MUSICAL FANFARE

Spotlight up

Announcer's Voice: "It's Showtime at the Sirocco Hotel."

On stage Clark Hamilton, with his guitar, sings:

(Music from "As Time Goes By")

"You must remember this,

Showtime must not be missed.

Dan Lewis where are you?..."

Suddenly, rushing into the room through a back door comes Dan Lewis. “Here I am, Here I am…”

As Lewis climbs up onto the stage Clark asks him, “Where the hell you been?”

“Thummy was watching a couple a kids.” Lewis held up his fist with “Thummy” extended.

“Watching kids? Clark shook his head… “That’s a reason to be late?”…

Nodding “yes,” Lewis looks down at Thumb . “You tell him..”

And Thumb begins to talk:

“We saw a little boy and girl playing in a sand box. The little boy said to the little girl, ‘I’ll show you mine if you show me yours.’

“So they to off their pants.

“The boy looked over at the girl; ‘Where’s your thing? He pointed to himself. Like mine.’

“She looks at his then said, ‘I don’t have one.’

“Well the boy started singin, ‘Mary’s got no thing, Mary’s got no thing…’ The little girl started crying and ran into the house.

“Five minutes later, all smiles, she came back out of the house. Making a face at the little boy she told him, ‘You only got one thing. Mommy says when I grow up, I can have as many as I want!”

Over the roar of crowd laughter, the announcer’s voice can be heard: “Ladies and Gentlemen, It’s Lewis and Clark.”

Seated at a front row table, Peter stops applauding and puts his hand on his wife's "What-a you think, Hon? Having fun?"

"Yes, I am. They are really funny. I think you owe Eve a huge bonus."

"Let's not go overboard Honey." Peter laughed as he got to his feet. "Come on. Let's go talk with them."

“**WHAT WOULD YOU THINK** about doing a monthly TV show?”

Dan blinked. Talk about surprises. He looked at his partner. For a change Clark’s facial expression showed some surprise too.

“You mean once a month, every month?” Clark asked.

“Yes.” Peter Best nodded his head up and down. “Chuck and Cathy want to ease up on their schedule next season. They want to cut down to every other week. You two could have one of the alternate weeks.”

“Who gets the other one?” Dan asked.

“Don’t know.” Peter leaned back in his chair and crossed his legs. “They haven’t told me that. I suppose they want to know about you guys first.”

“That sounds pretty....” Clark didn’t get to complete his sentence before Dan jumped in.

“Why don’t we alternate with them?”

Peter glanced at his wife and uncrossed his legs. “You mean every other week? You think you can come up with enough material for that?”

“Not by ourselves,” Dan answered. “But if you find us some good writers...”

“Sure, we can!” This time it was Clark’s turn to but in. “And when we can’t come up with something funny to do, I’ll sing.”

“He’ll sing?” Dan’s animated thumb appeared next to his ear.

“Over my dead body,” Dan told the hand. “Maybe we’ll both sing. Or better yet, maybe I’ll do a dance number.”

The hand looked shocked.

Clark looked shocked as well. “Good Lord. Better I should sing, believe me.”

“I go for that!” Marion’s enthusiastic comment was the first words she had spoken since she and Peter had said “hello” and sat down in the dressing room.

Laughing at his wife’s reaction, Peter shook his head. “Okay. Seriously, could you do a show every other week?”

“Seriously,” Clark answered, “We probably can, but it’s something Dan and I would have to think about.”

“That’s why we came to see you,” Peter said. “You don’t need to give them an answer right away, but you do need to think about it.”

“Peter...” Dan’s mind had already started to work on the idea. “We couldn’t do it without a lot of help. Writers, a director, a producer... People who understand our act, our material...”

“I agree with you on that...”

Before Peter could continue, Clark jumped in again. “Where would we do the show? New York?”

“No, I don’t think so. Chuck feels having his show coming from there and yours’ coming from LA would be better. He would have Broadway types for guests, you guys would have the pick of Hollywood."

"That makes a lot-a sense," Dan agreed.

"So where do we go from here?" Clark wanted to know.

"You two put your thinking caps on... See what ideas you come up with about format, that sort of thing. I'll put together a list of people you might like to work with."

"So what-a-ya think?" Dan returned his attention to his animated hand. "Sound exciting?"

Thumb nodded a vigorous "yes!"

PART III: Television Life

PETER BEST selected a writer named John Poer to produce the Lewis and Clark TV show. John, in turn, selected eight other writers to comprise the regular writing staff, and designated their office complex "The Poor House.

Among the writing staff were two young women named Anne: Anne Landry and Anne Bennett. Anne Landry quickly became "Al," and Anne Bennett "AB". Because AB seemed to have a flair for coming up with material for the talking thumb, she and Dan Lewis had become quite friendly.

One afternoon in the Poor House AB was going over a new routine:

You and thumb are leaning over the piano watching a guest lady play. We cut to her very pretty hands on the key board and focus in on her thumbs as they strike notes We cut to a closeup of Thumb watching. Back *to the keyboard as she finishes* … last note played by her thumb.

"Thumb looks up at you and tells you, 'I have got to hold hands with her.' Okay?"

Dan Lewis laughs and looks at the attractive young lady sitting next to him, "That's very good 'AB,'" he says, referring to Anne Bennett's nick-name.

"OK, thanks," she tells him. "Now can we get out of this studio, go to your place and get something to eat or do

I have to drive all the way to Encino in this pouring rain?"

The thought makes Dan blink.... "Ahh... yeah sure. Come on. I got a fridge full of food... we can find something."

Living alone, Dan had become a pretty good cook but as he watched her, he quickly realized she was much better at it. "You really know your way around a stove, Anne... I'm sorry. May I call you Anne rather than AB?"

"You certainly may." she told him. "And after we get in bed, I will love having you whisper Anne in my ear."

It was full daylight outside but he had no idea what time it was . All he knew for sure was he in bed, naked, with a naked woman next to him, and he had to pee. Before he could do anything, the naked lady jumped out of bed and hurried to the john saying, "I got-a pee" as she went.

He heard the john flush, then the shower start.

Moments later, bladder relieved, he joined the naked lady in the shower.

"A guy could get used to this sort of thing," he told himself. "Maybe it's time."

———

"Anne, if you would like to save your rent money, you could move in here with me."

"I like that idea." She kissed him on the ear. "We don't have to get married until the TV season ends next spring."

Dan Lewis blinked again then looked at his thumb, "You been pretty quiet, What-a you think?"

"You seem to be doing alright by yourself," Thumb answered. "Just make sure we honeymoon in the Catskills."

LADIES AND GENTLEMEN, Arronsteins proudly presents our outstanding graduate, television's own Dan Lewis.....

Loud applause from the packed audience welcome Dan as he and Anne walk out onto the stage.

"Welcome home, Dan," the announcer adds.

"Thank you. Thank you..." Dan waves and bows to the audience. "Thank you, thank you... May I introduce you to my beautiful wife, Anne."

More applause, even louder.

Then, as the applause dies down, Dan looks to his thumb. “You wanna say anything?”

“Yes. I do,” Thumb perks up. “As soon as you stop talking long enough for me to get a word in...”

Nodding courteously to Thumb, Dan tells him, “The mic is yours.”

Perking up and waving to the audience, Thumb clears his throat, then in his loudest voice,

“I want you to tell Anne and everyone how Eve turned the light on the chicken and the egg you and Clark left here in Aronsteins’ lobby.”

The End

www.ingramcontent.com/pod-product-compliance
Lightning Source LLC
Chambersburg PA
CBHW060603310726
48982CB00008B/1220/J

* 9 7 8 1 6 3 8 6 8 1 2 7 4 *